SHAPES AROUND ME

Triangles

Anita Loughrey

QED Publishing

What is a triangle?

A triangle has three straight edges and three corners.

Follow your finger around the edge of the triangle.

Which child is going to the triangle tent?

Susi   **Jane**   **Peter**

3

Counting triangles

Point to the triangles in the picture.

How many triangles
are there on each
of the lion's feet?

Answer: 6 triangles

How many triangle leaves does the tree have?

Answer: 10 triangles

Big and small

Triangles can be different sizes.

big

bigger

small

smaller

6

Look around your house. Can you find a big triangle shape?

biggest

smallest

Coloured triangles

Triangles can be different colours.

How many blue triangles can you see?

How many green triangles can you see?

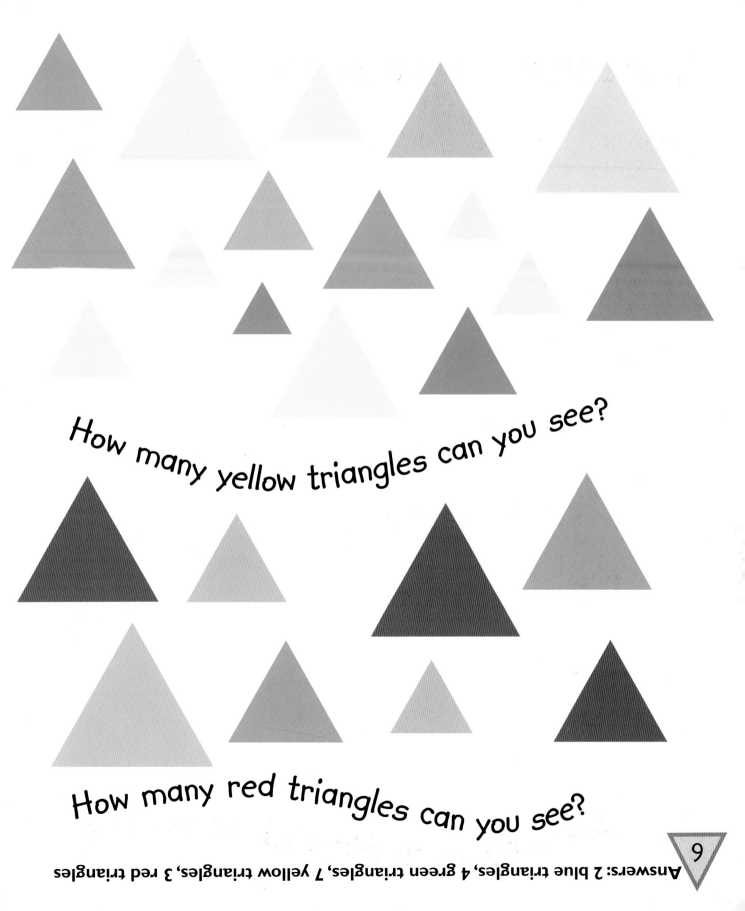

How many yellow triangles can you see?

How many red triangles can you see?

Answers: 2 blue triangles, 4 green triangles, 7 yellow triangles, 3 red triangles

Cat muddle!

Help the cat follow the path to get to the tree.

How many triangles
does the cat pass?

Look out of the
window. Point
to any
triangles
you can
see.

Answer: 7 triangles

Drawing triangles

Ask an adult to
help you to draw
this boat.

Ask an adult to
help you to draw
this kite.

At the lake

Point to all the triangles in the picture. Can you spot them all?

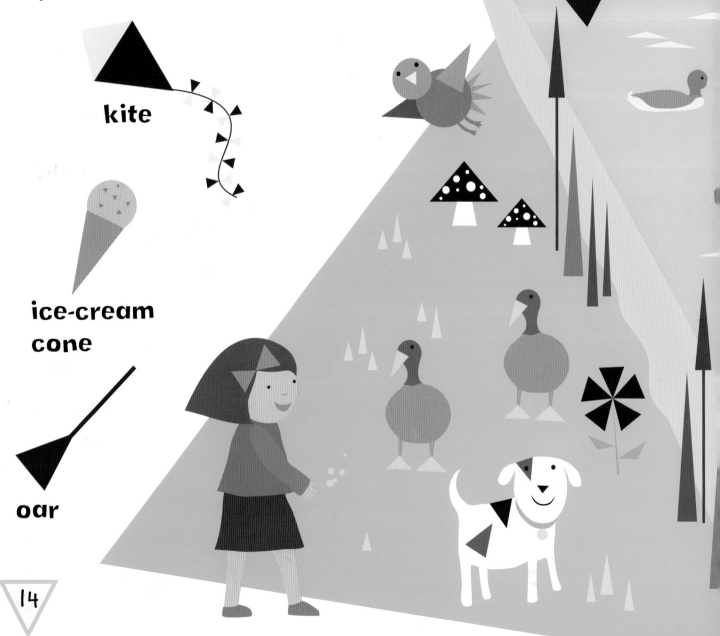

kite

ice-cream cone

oar

14

Which of these triangle shapes have you seen?

wing

hat

sail

15

At the mountains

Point to all the triangles in the picture. Which triangle is the smallest?

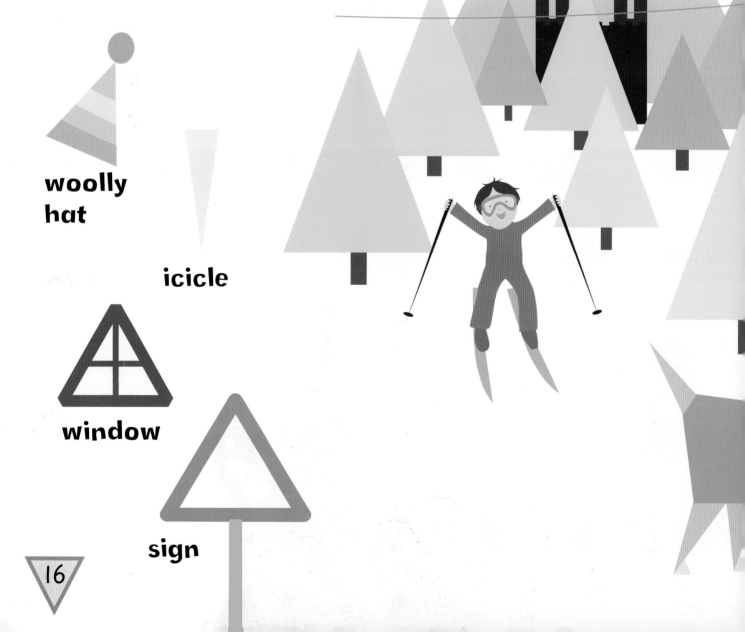

woolly
hat

icicle

window

sign

Have you seen trees shaped like triangles?

scarf

tree

bell

At the fairground

Point to all the triangles
in the picture. Can you
find more than ten
triangles?

flag

candyfloss

**giant
hammer**

tent

Hoopla

Coconut
Shy

Are flags always
a triangle
shape?

hoopla

popcorn

helter
skelter

Whirligig

Fortune
Teller

19

At the zoo

Point to all the triangles
in the picture.
Can you
find them all?

tooth

horn

20 **flipper**

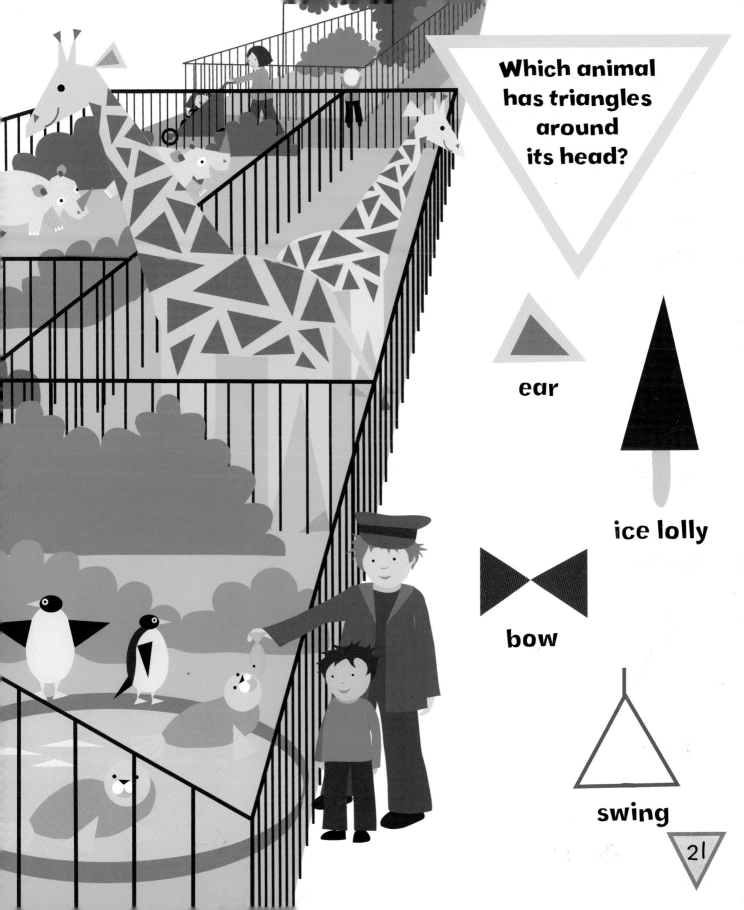

Which animal has triangles around its head?

ear

ice lolly

bow

swing

21

Going to a party

Point to all the triangles in the picture. Which ones have you seen at a party?

present

hat

cake

Which of these triangle foods have you eaten?

button

napkin

sandwich

pizza

Notes for parents and teachers

This book has been designed to help your child recognize triangles and to distinguish them from other shapes. The emphasis is on making learning fun, so the book uses the environment to reinforce what your child has seen in the book. The activities help your child to understand the idea of a triangle shape by using familiar, everyday objects.

Sit with your child and read each page to them. Allow time for your child to think about the activity. Encourage them to talk about what they see. Praise your child when they recognize the items shown in the book from their own experience. If any of the items are unfamiliar to your child, talk about them and explain what they are and where they might be found. Whenever possible, provide opportunities for your child to see the items in the everyday world around them.

Other activities for you to try with your child are:

✱ Play games such as, 'I spy with my little eye something triangle shaped that begins with...'.

✱ Cut out pictures of different-shaped objects from a catalogue and ask your child to sort them by shape, or to match them to pictures in this book.

✱ Encourage your child to look for things that are triangle shaped when you are out and about, or play this game at home.

✱ Let your child make collages or junk-models of different circle objects, or mould them in clay, so that they can explore the shape by touch.

Remember to keep it fun. Stop before your child gets tired or loses interest and try again another day. Children learn best when they are relaxed and enjoying themselves. It is best to help them to experience new concepts in small steps, rather than to try to do too much at once.

Illustrator Sue Hendra
Editor Amanda Askew
Designer Susi Martin

ISBN 978 1 84835 474 6

Printed and bound in China

Copyright © QED Publishing 2010

First published in the UK in 2010 by
QED Publishing
A Quarto Group company
226 City Road
London EC1V 2TT

www.qed-publishing.co.uk

A catalogue record for this book is available from the British Library.